This Walker book belongs to:

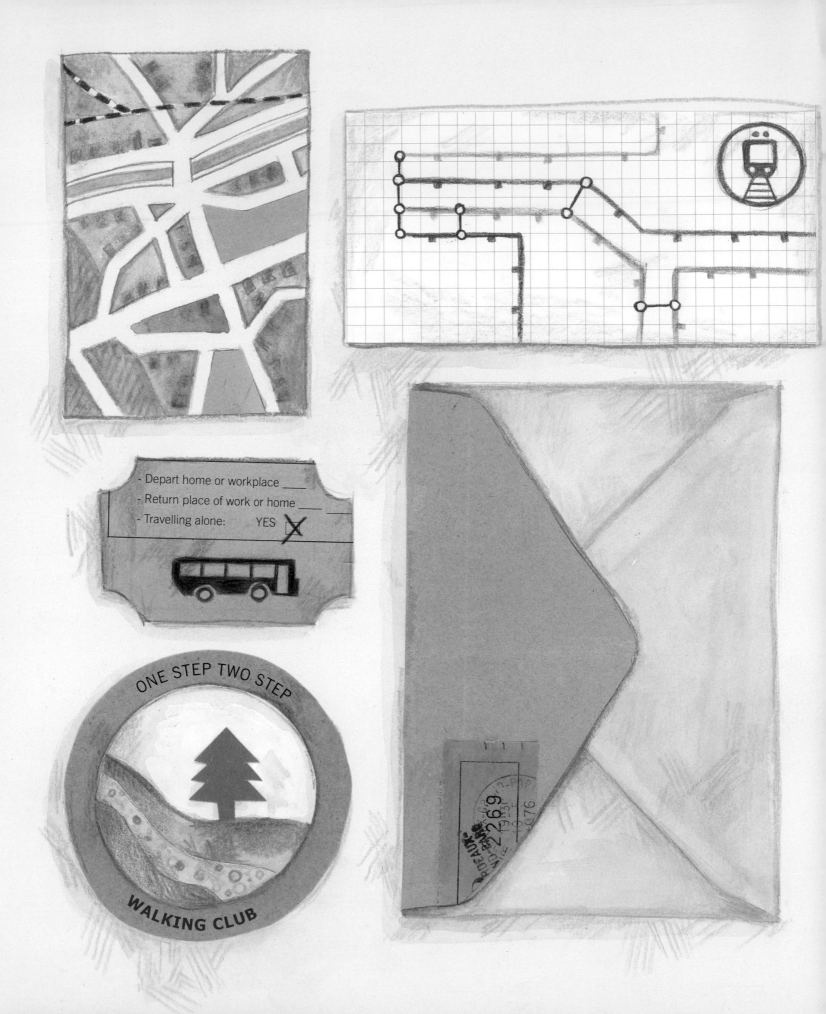

YOU ARE HERE

To: THE DODDS

From: RUDGE

For the love of travel and adventure

First published in Great Britain 2017 by Walker Books Ltd
87 Vauxhall Walk, London SE11 5HJ

10 9 8 7 6 5 4 3 2 1

© 2016 Leila Rudge

The right of Leila Rudge to be identified as the
author and illustrator of this work has been asserted by her
in accordance with the Copyright, Designs and Patents Act 1988

This book has been typeset in Mrs Eaves

Printed in China

British Library Cataloguing in Publication Data:
a catalogue record for this book is available from the British Library

ISBN 978-1-4063-6857-4

www.walker.co.uk

FSC
www.fsc.org
MIX
Paper from
responsible sources
FSC® C008047

Admit One

Gary

LEILA RUDGE

- Depart home or workplace ___
- Return place of work or home ___
- Travelling alone: YES   X

WALKER BOOKS
AND SUBSIDIARIES

LONDON • BOSTON • SYDNEY • AUCKLAND

Most of the time,
Gary was just like
the other racing pigeons.

He ate the same seeds.
Slept in the same loft.
And dreamt of adventure.

But on race days, when the pigeons set off in the travel basket, Gary stayed at home.

To pass the time, he organized his scrapbook.

He had a collection of travel mementos from everywhere.

Except Gary had never been anywhere.
Because Gary couldn't fly.

The racing pigeons usually returned just before supper.

And they always discussed wind directions and flight paths. Or waypoints.

Gary loved hearing about their adventures.

He would perch nearby and record everything in his scrapbook.

Until one night, Gary leaned a little too far.
And lost his balance.

His scrapbook flew up into the air.
Gary fell down to the bottom of the loft.

And they both
landed in the
travel basket
with a bump.

The next day was race day and Gary was a very long way from home.

By the time Gary woke up, the sky was full of feathers and flapping wings.

The racing pigeons were racing!

Except Gary didn't go anywhere —
because Gary couldn't fly.

Soon the other pigeons
were dots in the distance.

They were flying back
to the loft.

Gary wondered if
he would ever
find a way home.

Or if he would be lost in the city for ever.

ALL DIRECTIONS

STRAIGHT AHEAD

LEFT

RIGHT

RIGHT TURN
ONLY

FOLLOW
THE SIGNS

P

RAILWAY CROSSING A

Underground

nformation

Gary's collection
of travel mementos
always perked
him up. So he
opened up his
scrapbook.

Gradually, the city
came to feel a little
more familiar.

And Gary felt a
little less lost.

Before long, Gary had plotted his own way back to the loft.

Gary arrived home just before supper.
With all sorts of new travel mementos for his scrapbook.

And the most adventurous adventure story.
Gary couldn't fly. But Gary had been everywhere!

Most of the time, Gary was just
like the other racing pigeons.

He ate the same seeds.
Slept in the same loft.
And dreamt of adventure.

But on some days ...

the other pigeons were just like Gary.

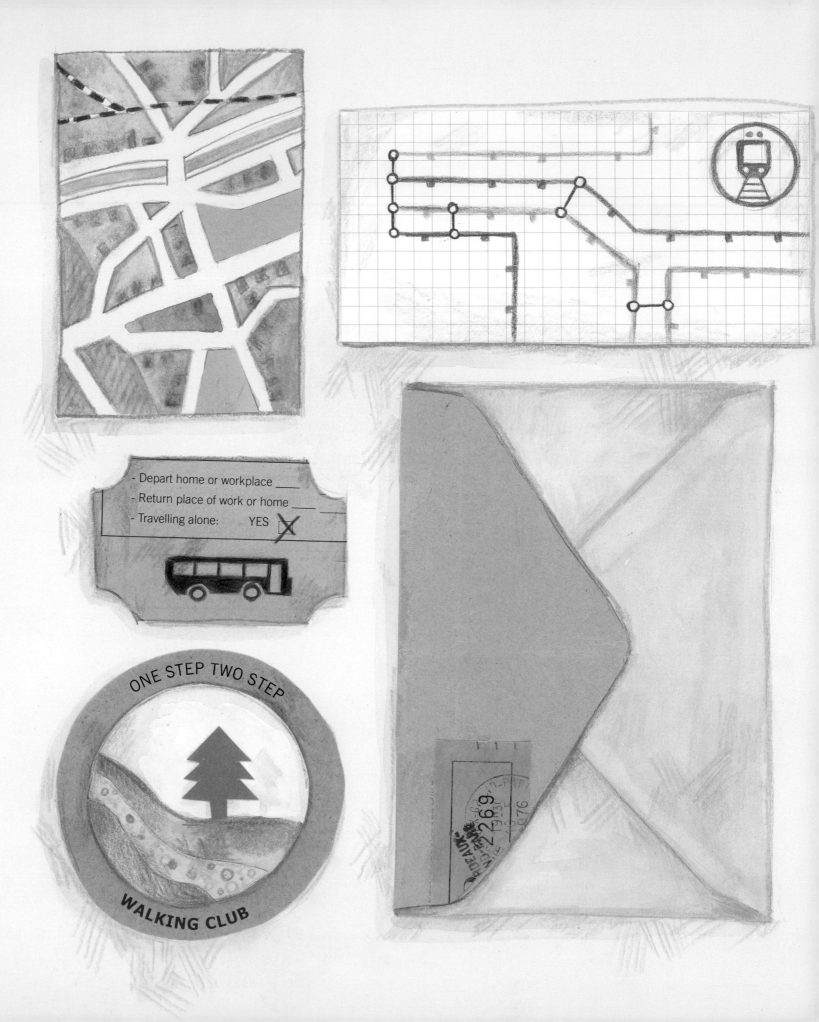

YOU ARE HERE

Departed
Arrived

21¢

УНІВЕРСINADA·1961

Belvidere

R353 BELVIDERE
78

DESTINATION: SOMEWHERE
ANY ROUTE PERMITTED

VALID FOR TRAVEL

Leila Rudge studied illustration at Bath Spa University before heading to Australia to seek her fortune (and the sunshine). She is the illustrator of *Mum Goes to Work*, written by Libby Gleeson, and the illustrator of *No Bears* and *Duck for a Day*, both written by Meg McKinlay. *A Perfect Place for Ted* was her authorial debut. Born in England and one of six siblings, Leila now lives in New South Wales, Australia with her husband and son.

Find Leila online at leilarudge.com and on Instagram as @leilarudge.

Look out for:

978-1-92152-982-5

Available from all good booksellers

www.walker.co.uk